A GOLDEN BOOK • NEW YORK

Library of Congress Control Number: 2008921461
ISBN: 978-0-375-84983-1
PRINTED IN SINGAPORE
10 9 8 7 6 5 4 3 2
First Random House Edition 2009

The Story of Jesus

By Jane Werner Watson · Illustrated by Jerry Smath

Jesus was born in Bethlehem, a town in the rocky
hills of Judea. Mary and Joseph were his parents.

Joseph worked as a carpenter. When Jesus grew old enough, he helped him.

Jesus was twelve years old when he and his parents went to Jerusalem for the feast of Passover. Jesus was thrilled by the sight of Jerusalem towering behind its great stone walls.

Jesus's heart rejoiced when he entered the temple,
the house of the Lord God. Jesus knew, even then,
that his life's purpose would be to work for his Father
in Heaven, telling people about Him.

When Jesus became a young man, he met a prophet called John the Baptist. John asked people to stop doing wrong and to be baptized to show that they were starting a new and better life.

John baptized Jesus in the River Jordan. At that moment, God sent a dove down from Heaven—a sign that He was pleased.

Afterward, Jesus went off by himself, deep
into the desert. He stayed for many days, thinking
about the good and evil in the world. He prayed for
God to show him the way to live his life.

When Jesus returned from the wilderness, he began to teach. He traveled from town to town, preaching the good news of the Kingdom of God and healing those who were sick.

Jesus met with fishermen
tending their nets on the shore . . .

and with shepherds
watching their flocks.

Once, Jesus spoke to a crowd of about five thousand people. It grew late and everyone was hungry. Only one boy had brought food—five loaves of bread and two small fishes.

Jesus took the boy's food and blessed it. Then he broke the food into pieces and gave it to the people. Through Jesus's miracle, everyone had enough to eat.

One night when Jesus and his disciples were
on a boat, a terrible storm blew up. The men were
terrified, but Jesus called out, "Quiet! Be still!"
The storm stopped, and the waves died down. This
was another one of Jesus's miracles.

Jesus often walked through vineyards and fields, teaching the people by telling them stories about people like themselves.

He told stories about workers gathering grapes in the vineyards, as Jesus gathered people to God. He told them about shepherds searching for lost sheep, as God searched for sinful people, hoping to change their ways. . . .

Jesus told people to follow the wishes of God rather than worry about becoming wealthy. He pointed to the flowers of the field, which do not worry about wealth or work for it. Yet God clothed them in greater beauty than wealth could ever buy.

But not everyone liked Jesus. The leaders of the temple were afraid that Jesus would turn the people against them. They were glad when a man named Judas offered to lead them to Jesus. The temple leaders paid Judas thirty pieces of silver.

Soon Jesus was captured by a group of soldiers. They brought him before the governor, a man named Pontius Pilate. When Judas saw this, he was sorry for what he had done to Jesus. He tried to return the money to the leaders of the temple, but it was too late.

Pontius Pilate let the soldiers take Jesus away to a place called Golgotha. There he was crucified with two other men. Before he died, Jesus prayed to God. "Forgive them," he said. It was a sad day for all the people who loved Jesus.

Three days later, some women visited
Jesus's tomb. They were surprised to find an
angel waiting for them. "Don't be afraid," the
angel said. "Jesus has risen! He is not here."

And soon Jesus appeared to the women
himself, on the road.

Just before Jesus went up to Heaven, he appeared to his disciples and told them to travel to faraway places and teach people to obey his words.

"And I will be with you always," promised Jesus, "until the end of the world."

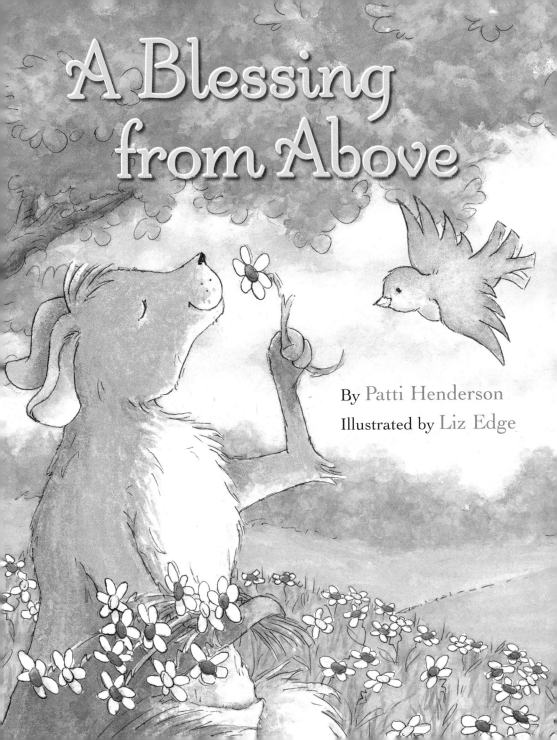

A Blessing from Above

By Patti Henderson

Illustrated by Liz Edge

Children are a gift from God; they are His reward.
— Psalm 127:3

Once upon a time there lived a mother kangaroo who had an empty pouch.

Every night before she went to sleep, she prayed that someday her pouch would be filled with a baby to love and hold and care for.

One day, Momma-Roo went for a walk.

Along the way, she saw a pair of butterflies fluttering about in a field of flowers.

She later came upon a mother duck leading her ducklings to a pond.

Next she spied a mama and papa squirrel
gathering acorns for their family.

She looked forward to the day she could share such wonderful sights and activities with a baby of her own.

Momma-Roo was getting tired. She decided to rest underneath the branches of a beautiful willow tree.

When she looked up she saw a bluebird nest stuffed full of baby bluebird eggs.

One by one, the eggs began to hatch.
The baby bluebirds stretched their wings and cried
for food.

The nest was getting very crowded.

Just as the last and littlest bluebird cracked
open his shell and stepped into this world . . .

. . . one of his brothers stretched his wings for the first time.

Before the littlest one knew what was happening, he was bumped from the nest and falling . . .

down,

down,

down . . .

. . . straight into Momma-Roo's pouch!

The baby bluebird peeked out from the pouch
and gazed up at Momma-Roo.
"Hello, Mommy," he chirped.

The mother bluebird looked down and saw her littlest one.

She knew her nest was not big enough for all her chicks. It made her happy to see her baby in such a warm, cuddly place.

"Hello, Little One," said Momma-Roo.

Then she hugged her blessing from above.
"At last! My very own baby!" she cried joyfully.
"I will cherish you and love you forever!"

On their way back home, Momma-Roo and
Little One frolicked through the field of flowers.

They stopped for a sip of water at the pond.

They shared grass and berries with each other.
They were so happy!

Now, every night before they fall asleep,
Momma-Roo and Little One thank God for all
their blessings . . . but especially for each other.

In love He destined us
for adoption to Himself. . . .
—Ephesians 1:5

My Little Golden Book About
GOD

By Jane Werner Watson • *Illustrated by* Eloise Wilkin

GOD IS GREAT.

Look at the stars in the evening sky,
so many millions of miles away
that the light you see shining left its star
long, long years before you were born.

Yet even beyond the farthest star,
God knows the way.
Think of the snow-capped mountain peaks.
Those peaks were crumbling away with
age before the first people lived on earth.
Yet when they were raised up sharp and new
God was there, too.

Bend down to touch the smallest flower.
Watch the busy ant tugging at his load.
See the flash of jewels on the insect's back.
This tiny world your two hands could span,
like the oceans and mountains and far-off stars,
God planned.

Think of our earth, spinning in space

so that now, for a day of play and work
we face the sunlight, then we turn away—

to the still, soft darkness for rest and sleep.
This, too, is God's doing.

For GOD IS GOOD.

God gives us everything we need—
shelter from cold and wind and rain,
clothes to wear and food to eat.

God gives us flowers, the songs of birds,
the laughter of brooks, the deep song of the sea.

He sends the sunshine

to make things grow,

sends in its turn
the needed rain.

God makes us grow, too, with minds and eyes
to look about our wonderful world,
to see its beauty, to feel its might.

He gives us a small, still voice in our hearts
to help us tell wrong from right.
God gives us hopes and wishes and dreams,
plans for our grown-up years ahead.

He gives us memories of yesterdays,
so that happy times and people we love
we can keep with us always in our hearts.
For GOD IS LOVE.

God is the love of our mother's kiss,

the warm, strong hug of our daddy's arms.

God is in all the love we feel
for playmates and family and friends.

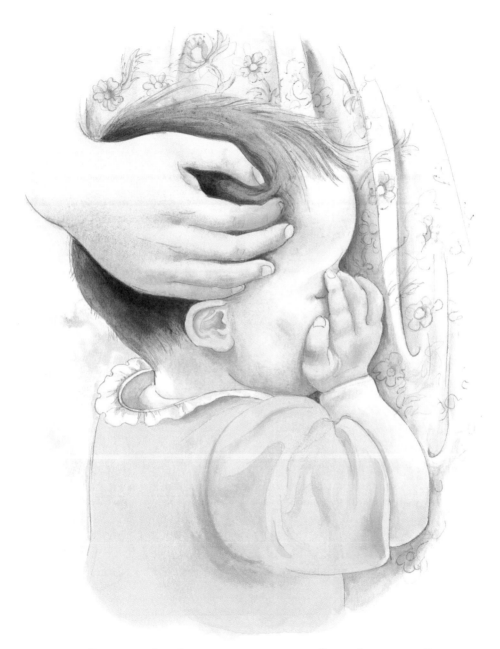

When we're hurt or sorry or lonely or sad,
if we think of God, He is with us there.

God whispers to us in our hearts:
"Do not fear, I am here,
And I love you, my dear.
Close your eyes and sleep tight,
For tomorrow will be bright—
All is well, dear child.
Good night."